REDNECK™

CREATED BY
Donny Cates & *Lisandro Estherren*

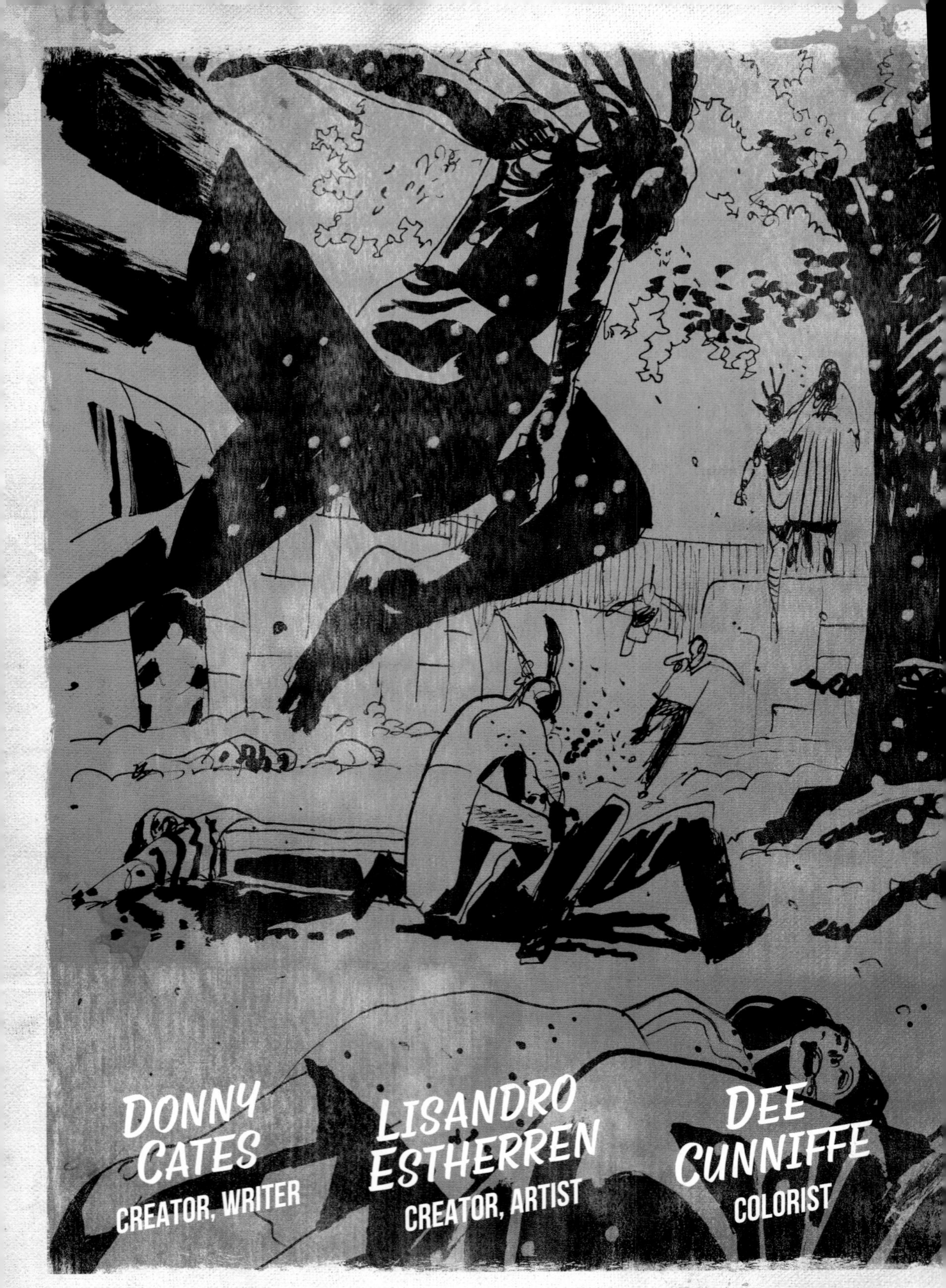

REDNECK VOLUME 5. FIRST PRINTING. APRIL 2021. ISBN: 978-1-5343-1609-6 PUBLISHED BY IMAGE COMICS, INC. OFFICE OF PUBLICATION: PO BOX 14457, PORTLAND, OR 97293.

PRINTED IN THE U.S.A.

SKYBOUND LLC. *ROBERT KIRKMAN* CHAIRMAN *DAVID ALPERT* CEO *SEAN MACKIEWICZ* SVP, EDITOR-IN-CHIEF *SHAWN KIRKHAM* SVP, BUSINESS DEVELOPMENT *BRIAN HUNTINGTON* VP, ONLINE CONTENT *SHAUNA WYNNE* SR. DIRECTOR, CORPORATE COMMUNICATION *ANDRES JUAREZ* ART DIRECTOR *ARUNE SINGH* DIRECTOR OF BRAND, EDITORIAL *ALEX ANTONE* SENIOR EDITOR *JON MOISAN* EDITOR *ARIELLE BASICH* ASSOCIATE EDITOR *CARINA TAYLOR* GRAPHIC DESIGNER *JOHNNY O'DELL* SOCIAL MEDIA MANAGER *DAN PETERSEN* SR. DIRECTOR, OPERATIONS & EVENTS FOREIGN RIGHTS I& LICENSING INQUIRIES: CONTACT@SKYBOUND.COM WWW.SKYBOUND.COM

IMAGE COMICS, INC. *ROBERT KIRKMAN* CHIEF OPERATING OFFICER *ERIK LARSEN* CHIEF FINANCIAL OFFICER *TODD MCFARLANE* PRESIDENT *MARC SILVESTRI* CHIEF EXECUTIVE OFFICER *JIM VALENTINO* VICE PRESIDENT *ERIC STEPHENSON* PUBLISHER/CHIEF CREATIVE OFFICER *NICOLE LAPALME* CONTROLLER *LEANNA CAUNTER* ACCOUNTING ANALYST *SUE KORPELA* ACCOUNTING & HR MANAGER *MARLA EIZIK* TALENT LIAISON *JEFF BOISON* DIRECTOR OF SALES & PUBLISHING PLANNING *DIRK WOOD* DIRECTOR OF INTERNATIONAL SALES & LICENSING *ALEX COX* DIRECTOR OF DIRECT MARKET SALES *CHLOE RAMOS* BOOK MARKET & LIBRARY SALES MANAGER *EMILIO BAUTISTA* DIGITAL SALES COORDINATOR *JON SCHLAFFMAN* SPECIALTY SALES COORDINATOR *KAT SALAZAR* DIRECTOR OF PR & MARKETING *DREW FITZGERALD* MARKETING CONTENT ASSOCIATE *HEATHER DOORNINK* PRODUCTION DIRECTOR *DREW GILL* ART DIRECTOR *HILARY DILORETO* PRINT MANAGER *TRICIA RAMOS* TRAFFIC MANAGER *MELISSA GIFFORD* CONTENT MANAGER *ERIKA SCHNATZ* SENIOR PRODUCTION ARTIST *RYAN BREWER* PRODUCTION ARTIST *DEANNA PHELPS* PRODUCTION ARTIST WWW.IMAGECOMICS.COM

SKYBOUND

image

*"There are those whose teeth are swords,
whose fangs are knives, to devour the poor
from off the earth, the needy from mankind."*

Proverbs 30:14

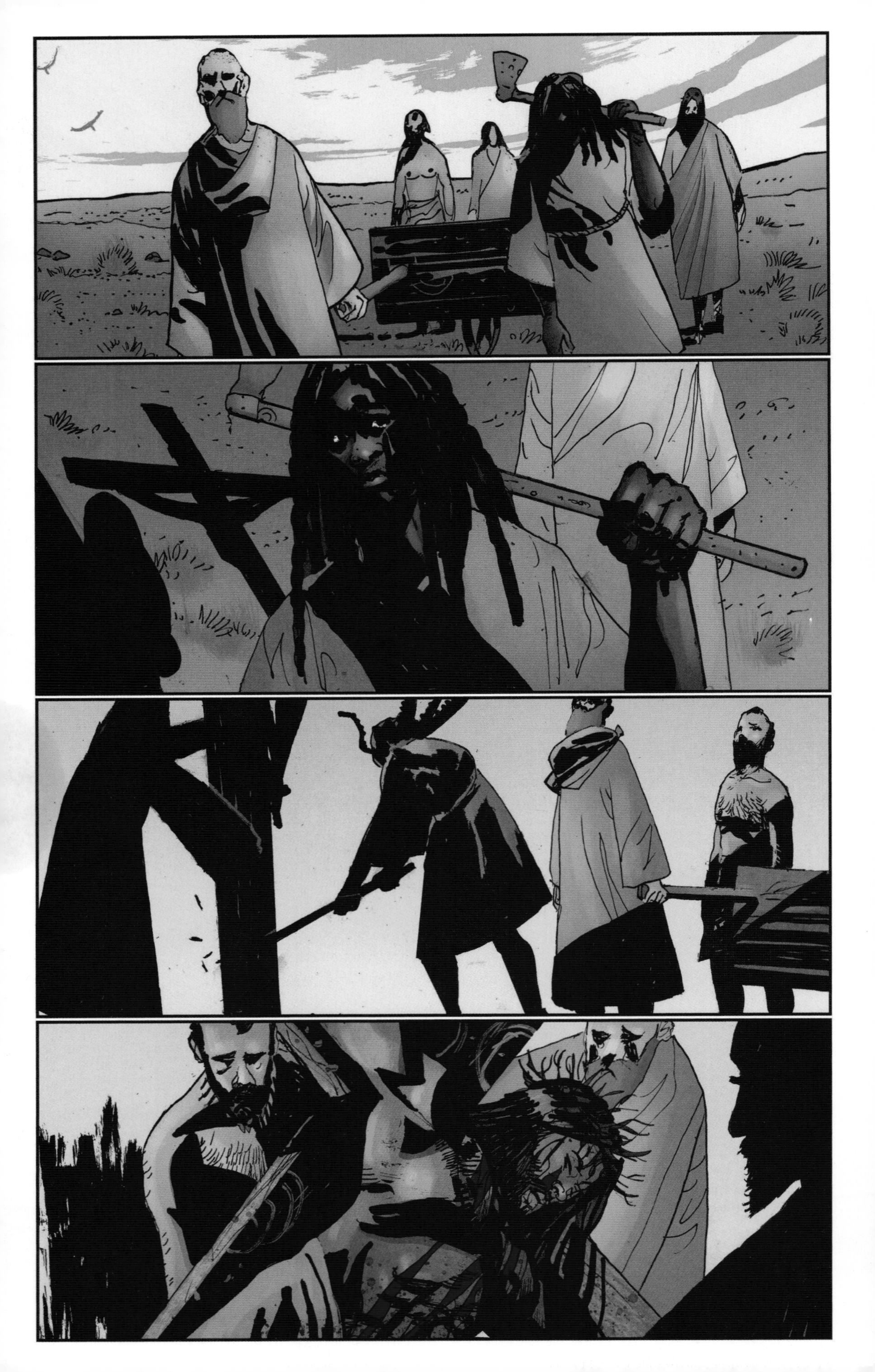

"For the life of every creature is its blood: its blood is its life. Therefore, I have said to the people of Israel, you shall not eat the blood of any creature, for the life of every creature is its blood. Whoever eats it shall be cut off."

Leviticus 17:14

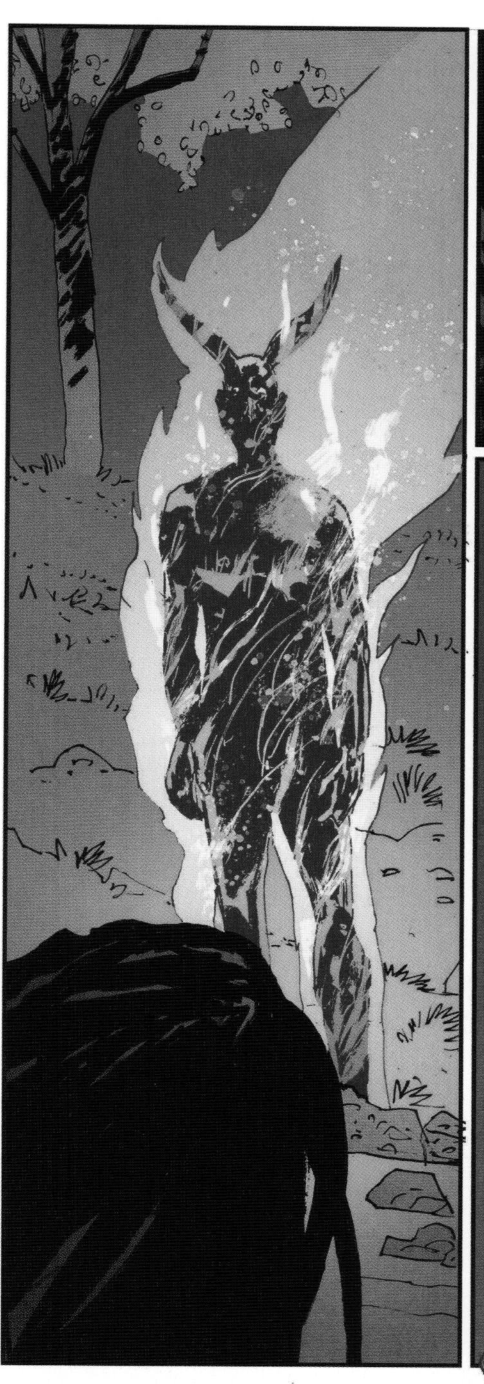

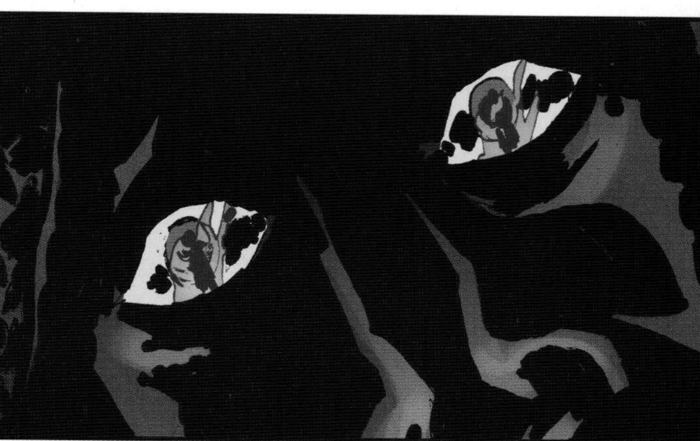

"Whoever eats my flesh and drinks my blood has eternal life, and I will raise him up at the last day."

John 6:54

"...give no opportunity
to the devil."

Ephesians 4:27

"And in those days people will seek death and will not find it...

"They will long to die, but death will flee from them."

Revelation 9:6

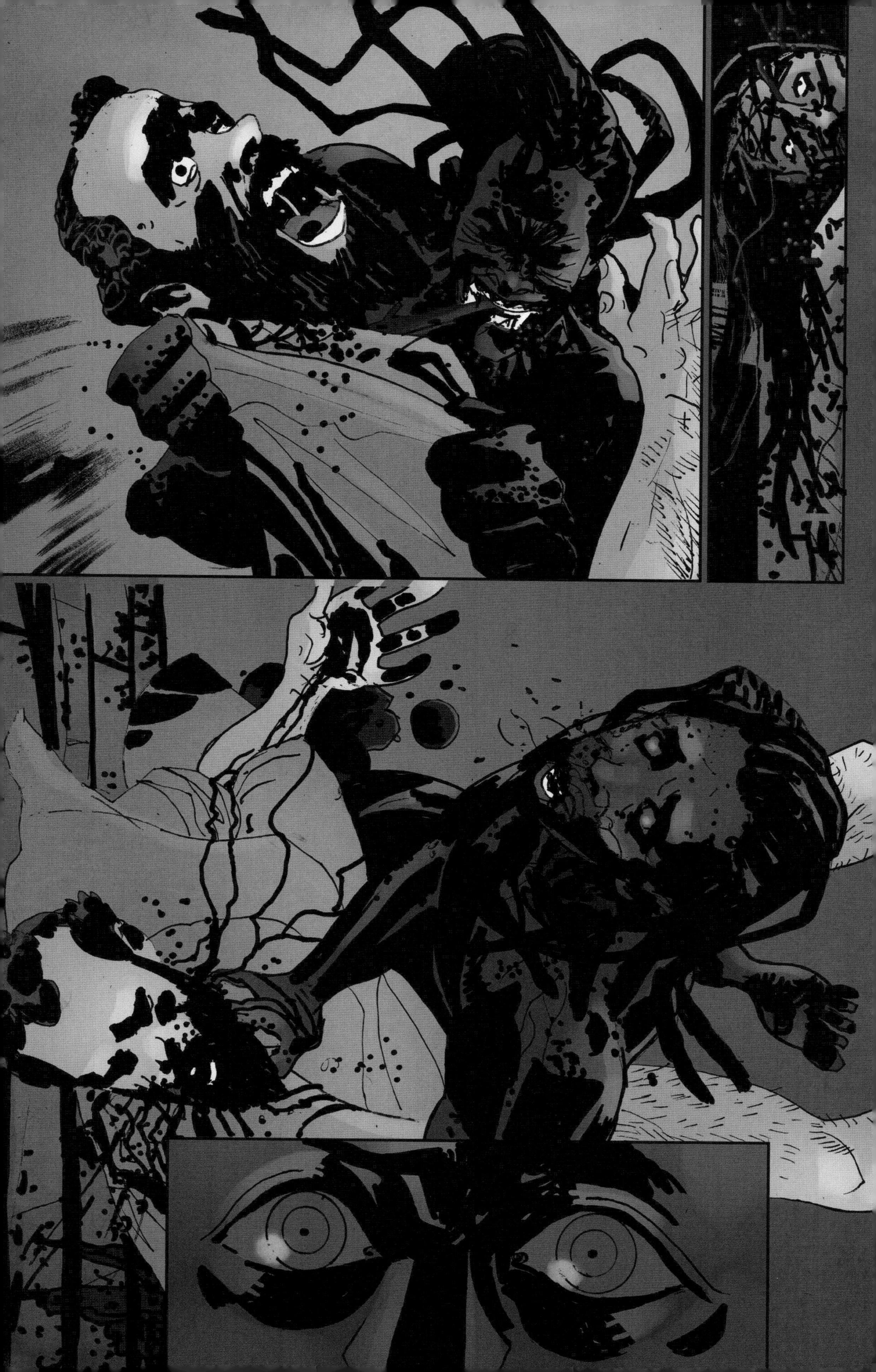

Do you want to see more?
...Yes.

How the fuck are you still alive?

Heh.
Well. I... assume you mean that little affair with the police of Sulphur Springs, yes?
Where you burst into flames after being shot in the face by Uncle Bartlett a half-dozen times?
Yeah...
Yeah, that'd be the one.
Mphf.
You have so much to learn, boy.

Demus.
He made you this monster.
Oh.
I was a monster long before I was a vampire, child.
Fuck that. You think you can come back like this and I'm supposed to forget what you did?
If I want you to, yes.
He's your sire, isn't he?
But there will be time for that later...
You asked me a question.

"I saved our family that day in Sulphur Springs, boy.
"You may disagree with my methods...
"My motivations...
"But you have benefitted greatly from my actions.
"All of you.
POLICE
"But...you have suffered in my wake, as well.
"At the hands of humans...
"At the hands of those I warned against...those I *warred* against...
"And yet, I am remembered as a villain.

"If I am...
remembered
at all.
"You left
me there.
"To rot.
To die.
"Alone...in the ashes
of the kingdom I
built for you.
"But I was
not forgotten...
"Not by
all...

"He found me. And he...
No...
Please... release me...
No, child...
"...He saved me."
We are not done yet.

Like he will save you.
Like he will save all of us.

Whether we are worthy of it or not!
Agh!

You know what, old man? I don't give a rat's ass who the fuck you think you are, no one--
Enough!

Put your teeth away.

Both... of you.

Follow me, boy.

To the... gardens.

"I drank...of the blood of the Lamb.
"And His father, our God...cursed me to walk these lands forever...untouched by His grace or...the light of his sun...
"Cursed...to never know the salvation of the cross...
"And so...I burden myself as He. Burning His sign to my flesh to...atone...
"For what I have done. And what I will do...
"I...I was the first.
"The dawning of that which you know..."

...As vampire.
That's...
Fuck.
...Yes.
I...imagine this must be... quite a lot...for one so... young.
I...I have so many questions. I feel like...I don't know. My head is racing and...
How? I mean...
How did you get here?
A boat.
...What?
A rather... large boat.

The Black Sea.
1449.
"There were many more dawns between... this and the last, much more blood.
"But none of them... matter. And all of them...have faded.
"What is...important, is that this was the beginning...of my great crusade.
"When I preached the gospel...of unending life across the world to any who would...see the path...

"That we needn't be... beholden to God's ill-thought... plan any longer.
"That we could be...free.
"In those days I had...but one general at my side.
"A Norse woman. The matriarch...of the lost Viking horde I had turned in...my travel. The last of her kind.
"Ingrid...was her name. I believe you knew her."
Land ahead.
Trouble, as well.

Man.
SNIP
As we grew... as my hordes began to swallow the horizon...from every corner of the world...
Man... began...to see us.
Such a... primitive kind... unable to see...the gift...I would bring them. Unable to veer from the path of the... maker.
War was... of course... inevitable.
The wars, yeah...yeah, my dad always talked about those. Or, well...he wouldn't say much, but...
He was there, right? My dad?
Ah. Johann. The Dark One.
Heh...His story would... come later, child.

"Johann"?
The war would last...centuries, boy. And in those times, we faced scores of men that we turned to our cause.
Generals, armies, kings, emperors and great tyrants...
All fell to my... promise.
And then... there was another...
One day...
We met a monster.

"He was a warrior born of the devil, they say. Ruthless... and...bloodthirsty.
"Like an animal.
"A demon born in man's flesh, they would say.
"Cast out of Hell...to send God's enemies back from whence he was delivered.

"We would not... survive this man's wrath.
"None who ever faced him...did.
"They called him the Son of the Dragon.

"Vladimir Tepes the Third.
"Dracul.
"The Impaler."

<Nicodemus.>
<Join me, won't you?>

Wait...
Yes... wonderful, is it not?
Our... history...
Vladimir taught us... so much.
Military... tactics... stratagems... survival.
Survival at all costs.
He gave us...everything. This very castle, in fact.
And...in turn...
I gave him the night.

Okay. Fuck.
Hold on.
So... you're telling me...you're being serious? You're talking about--
Oh... yes.
Sometimes legends...live to tell truth.
You're talking about fucking *Dracula*, right?!
We're in Dracula's castle?
You knew
DRACULA?!
Yes, of course, Gregory...

And so...do you.

"In the winter of 1587, every man, woman and child in the settlement of Roanoke Island disappeared without a trace.
"The story of what happened to these settlers has long remained a mystery in the halls of man.
"But we...
"We are not men.

"For months, the cold had descended on them.
"Crops dying. Children starving.
"Hunters leaving the camp never to return. Their bodies never found...

"Wolves howling in the night.
"Strange fingernail scratches on the walls surrounding the colony.
"Someone, or something, wanted in, they would say.

"Some suspected the Devil.
"Talk of witches in the darkness.

"And so it was that a party of four starving and ill-equipped men left the walled colony...

"To bring food.
"To kill the wolves.

"To face the Devil."
There.
You see how they circle...
Something has died.
If we follow them we may--
John!
In the trees!
<Please! Help me!>

<Run! Run! There are demons in the wind! Please! They killed them! They eat the children!!! Please, you must turn back!>
What is he saying?! Why is he screaming?!
Stay back! Stay back, damn you!
<They are coming! Please, listen to me! You must go back! This is a land of death! There is no place to hide, you must-->
BOOM
BOOM

Goddamn you...
Leave it be, John. They carry disease. It could be--
No. He was running from something, Jacob. He's bleeding.
Look here. Something has bitten him. It...
What is it? A wolf bite?
...I...
I do not know.
I have never seen wounds of this kind.
And the rifle shot... it doesn't bleed.
This... this man has no blood in him.
Jacob, we need to return to camp. I fear this could...

Jacob?

Jacob!!!
Thomas, Caleb! Come out!
Jacob!!!

FWISH
"The demons, as they called them, in the woods of Roanoke were unlike any native tribe the men of the New World would ever encounter...
Jacob! Son, please! Follow my voice if you can--
"But, they did share one very important tradition...
God in Heaven...

"They used every part of the animals they killed."

...Empty... where are the...
Oh...oh Lord...
The camp!!!

HAAAAAA!!

Agh!!!

N-No!!!
Get back!
No,
I-I revoke
thee!!!
Aghh!!!
It-it
cannot be
you!!! Speak
your name!
"And the
Burning Man
spoke.
Say it!!!
Say your
name!!!
"And he who man calls
the Fallen One. Satan,
Lucifer or the Devil
Himself did, in fact,
speak his true name...

"And with his last burning breath, the last settler of the colony of Roanoke carved that name into the breast of an oak for all to see the truth."
CROATOAN

Though no man...that has ever seen it... has known what the word means...
And now you do.
Why...
I can't...
I mean... I'm sorry, how do you even know this is true? None of you were there...

Watch your mouth, you little--
Vladimir, please. It is... good...that he challenges... what...he is... told.

I don't mean to be disrespectful, but I mean, aren't there... records or something? Like a...I don't know, a book or--
All things men make fade and die. Ink and paper turn to fire and dust.
Records are impermanent.

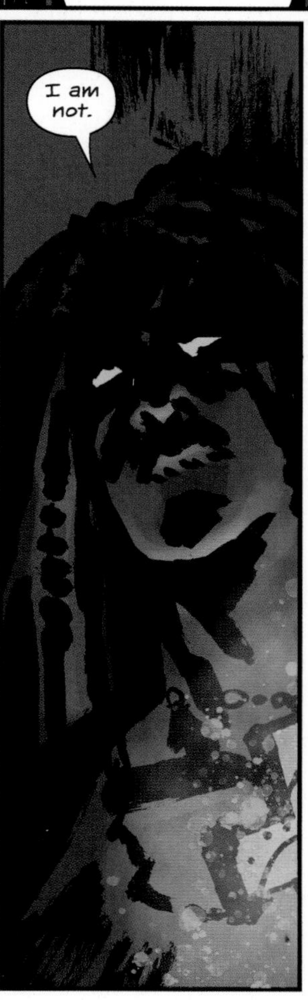
I am not.

"But...to answer your...question, we know these things because we...landed on the shores of the New World the following year.
"You see, the Burning Man made me. And in turn, I made all of you...
"We had not been to this New World...
"But when we arrived...
"Their hordes had swallowed the horizon.

"They knew us as their kind at once.
"And of me, they sensed something... familiar...
"A child of the Burning Man.
"And so...they took us to the one they worshipped.
"The one they knew as their vampire god.
"The one...we cannot...explain...
"My shadow...
"The only other vampire born of the Burning Man...
"He has had many names...

"Johan.
"Johnson Vladimir Bowman.
"You call him father...
"They called him the Dark One."
LISANDRO ESTHERREN

Asilo Del Muerto.
Mexico.
Now.
Well, hell. Guess it's been a while since I picked up this ol' journal.
Hadn't really had much time to write in it since we took over Asilo.
And, well, if I'm being honest, since I was reawoken or reborn or whatever, and what with the war and after the revolution...
Things ain't really changed that much since I started this thing in Sulfur Springs, anyhow.
JV's the mayor now. I guess that's diffrent.
Though you wouldn't know it by the way he goes about conducting his business.
As for me?

Some idiot mayor elected me sheriff of this here hellhole.
Which, I guess... I'm skipping a coupla' things. As I'm wont to do.
First thing I suppose I should address is my current state of dress, as July had commented on my sudden change after my second (third?) resurrection.
When I was reborn, I had the power of a newly sired vampire. And sired by an Elder, to boot.
But, well, me not being a vampire-born like JV, that new strength and power tended to fade with time.

I'm still stronger'n shit. But the wings? I cut them things off myself. They itched like shit and the only other of my kin who had them wasn't exactly the best branch of an already rotten tree.
So. Here I am. Sheriff Bartlett of the Asylum of the Dead. King shit of a kingdom of death. Hoo-rah.
I'm trying like hell to not look backwards anymore. That way lies ruination and regret...but...

Honestly, I look through these pages... the ones where I wasn't there...reading them places where July wrote to me while I was gone...
Night, Sheriff.
Have you a good one, Daryl. You take it easy on them cards, now, you hear me?
Hehe, yes, sir. Yes, sir.

...They hurt to read. But I'll be damned if they don't make me happier than hell to be back.
And as fragile and hopefully temporary as our current situation is.
Instead of runnin' and hiding and fightin' and dying for all these years on behalf of other folks...
I think I finally found myself something to **live for**.
Speaking of which...

If you wouldn't mind not drinking blood in the dark for a moment.
This one needs changing.
Her name is Mary.
Heh. Yessir, boss.
Meredith Bartlett Elinore Bowman.
(The Elinore part was July's mother's name. And yeah, she ain't really a Bowman. Just like I'm not. But it just...seemed right.)
Come here, baby.
Now, Perry, what I tell you about reading my mind while I'm on duty?
Hey, come on. Little ears, man.
What duty? Nothing happens here. It's boring as shit.
We're all Bowmans now.
I have been inside Mary's head more times than I can count.
To calm her. To help her sleep.
Her mind is mostly the colors of sunset, the sense of velvet. A small, but growing orbit of scents and sounds of you and July, that revolve around an ever-dimming echo of a distant heartbeat.
It is, in fact, the most beautiful place my mind has ever touched. But I promise you...
She has no idea what the fuck we are saying.

All of us. Together.
Oh, Perry, honey, give her to me and let your uncle work.
July, it's fine. I don't mind. Hell, Perry's right. I'm not doing anything anyhow.
No, I'll take her. Is JV done bleeding the cattle? I have to feed Mary in a bit and--
Yup. I'll go find him. Y'all go on inside.

Living in hell and happier'n a pig in shit.
Thank you, Sheriff.
My absolute pleasure, ma'am.
I love you.
I love you right back.

All of us...
Evil. Hang back a sec, yeah?

Except one...
You got anything for me?

NO SIGN OF HIM
SORRY. I'LL KEEP TRYING-

Except.
One.
Goddammit. Keep looking...

I wanna know where the fuck Greg is.

Agh!!!

Slow! Slow, Gregory!
I'm moving as fast as I can, dammit!

No! Your mind!!!

Slow mind. Quick hands.

That is how you win.

How we will all win.

Against who? Against what?
All you ever do is tell me stories. All I ever do is train and listen! What the fuck are we doing?

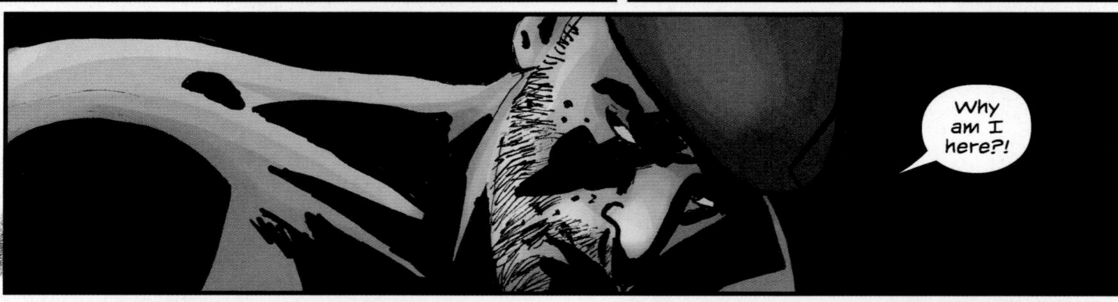
Why am I here?!

You are in training to be a leader, boy. To take your place in history...
As we take ours back.
The Parliament. The humans. The world...

You are here...to help us bleed them all.

Austin, Texas. 1884.
"To understand why you are here, you must know how we have come to our place in history.
"To understand the Parliament. And the wars.
"It began after we emerged from our caves, when men arrived and settled the land we had chosen as our new kingdom.
"A place called Texas.
C. J. MARTIN
HOTEL

"These men. These new men. They came in droves and they slaughtered our kind like cattle.
"Vampire or not, they dwindled our horde and our prey more each day, through disease and technology, as they continued to build their mortal empire on the bones of our own.
"We brought this new land the gift of everlasting life.
"But these men...they saw no value in any life, save their own...

"There were five of us that led our withering pack in those days.
Take as many as you can and get out quickly. Scatter when you do.
If they track us home, we will not want that fight.

"Ingrid, my oldest and most loyal. My Viking general.
I'll flank the left. Cover the exits and alleys.

"Carroña. Our newest and youngest member of the pack. *'El halcón mexicano.'* He was useful in gathering the vampires from Mexico.
"But much, much too wild in those days.
And I have the right. Drive them into the center of town and feast, *eh?*

"Vladimir, and myself, of course...
Careful, Carroña. Slow...minds. Quick hands.
Breathe, child...this is not a culling. Not yet.

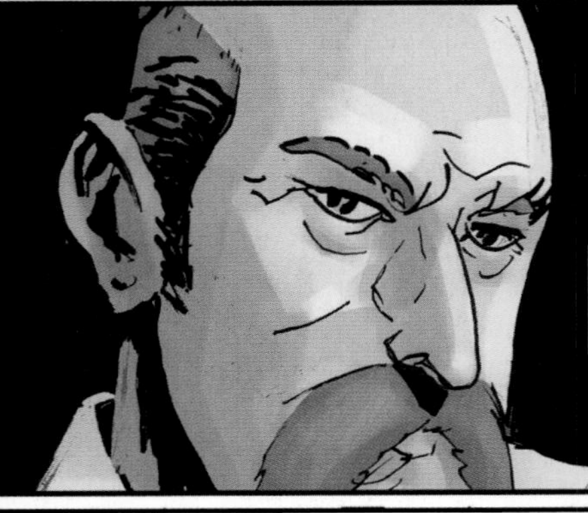
"And then there was your father. In those days he had been taken under the wing of Vladimir. And we had given the dark one a name.
"*Johan Vladimir.*
"I chose the name Johan. For his ***fire-born*** miracle of an existence was truly a gift from God.
"Your grandfather insisted on the second.
"The Bowman part would come later.

There has to be another way...

What does that mean, son?
This. Nightly raids...taking settlers at night...fightin' and dying.
We have to do better. This ain't sustainable. We have to change. Come up with something else...hell, there's buffalo everywhere. We could maybe--
Johan, we are...taking back what is ours. We will not feed like... animals. It is not our way.
Well *"our way"* ain't working for shit! We need to--

Shut your mouth, boy. Demus has spoken.
Now ride or starve. But I will not hear that talk from you again.

"I knew...in that moment, that your father and I were part of a...larger game.
"One that would only ever end...
You got something to say to me?

"At the other one's throat.
Didn't think so.

"But then, after this...
"The first light of what would become...our undoing began to rise...
"The Parliament. The trial. The war...

BLOOD! BLOOD!
THURSDAY NIGHT'S HORR
BLE BUTCHERY.
THE DEMONS HAVE TRANSFERRED
THEIR THIRST FOR BLOOD
TO WHITE PEOPLE.
"The Servant Girl Annihilator..."

This.
This is not what we do!!!
Not like this, Vladimir!!!
I killed some whores, who cares? I was bored and I--

You mutilated them. You... left them. They have witnesses. They know you. And I did not sanction these killings! You will not--

You won't *what?* You remember, you came to *me* for help!
You came to me to help you win *your crusade* and when you start to lose, *I'm* the one who is out of line?
This is not who we are!
To hell with you!

Demus... sire, I am sorry.
I...I am just so tired of these men and this hiding.
I promise you I won't--
No. You won't.
First nightfall, I want you on a boat to London.
I have formed a network of our kind around the globe.
A parliament. To take action against the growing tide of man. If you are so bored here, then perhaps you can be of service elsewhere...
If you wish to prove yourself to me, you will act as our liaison there.

When, and if, you can show to me that you can behave...
You may come back.
I...
London...

It will be... my honor to represent you, Lord Demus.
And you have my word...

London. 1888.
"I will make you proud."
Vladimir Tepes. Lord Dracul...
You have been charged by this Parliament as a danger to the security and ongoing survival of our species as a whole...
And by the powers entrusted to me by the fire-born king, I find you guilty.
With a sentence of death to be administered by way of--
Lord Frost...
That will not be necessary.
I will take Vladimir back with me.
Lord Demus. We...were not expecting you.
I speak on behalf of this council that it is an honor to have you in our chambers.

The honor is mine, Lord Frost. I am impressed with how you have... grown...in this place.
Guard, please remove the prisoner's chains. I will be taking--
Belay that order, guard. You will stand down.
Lord Demus, while your presence here commands the highest of respect...
Your orders in this council do not supersede those of the Parliament.
With due respect, the prisoner has been sentenced to death. And that is the final judgment.
You... insolent...
I formed this Parliament. I am the first born of our kind, lord and father to every vampire on Earth, and the sire of this prisoner.
Vladimir is leaving here with me, child.
How many of your soldiers and members of your own council die in that process is up to you.
"And with a word..."
...Guards?

"War.
"The Parliament led a revolt against me.
"Against its own kind.

"Instead of building towards the future I had always dreamed of...of bringing the gift of life to the world...
"We found ourselves fighting one another for years. For decades.
"Eventually, their numbers... consumed us.
"We were pushed back across the ocean...
"But not to lick our wounds...
"No..."

To plan. To think. To build.
I sent Vladimir back to Texas...under the care of Johan.
I had... hoped that your father would carry on our cause. To help...grow our numbers.
Instead, he...turned his back on me. On our family.
Eventually, word came that he had abandoned us entirely. That he had locked Vladimir in a cage and taken the surname of ***a...woman***.
Her name was Meredith. She was my mother.
Not anymore.

Now you have no mother. No father. Save one...
Now you are an orphan prince and a general of my armies.
Gregory...
It is time.

Will you renounce the Bowman name?
Will you meet your own blood on the battleground?

Yes, my lord.

No!
Agh!

Say it again.

Yes.
Father.

Well done, my son. You may rise.
You have listened. You have learned. You have trained.
You have renounced the traitorous name of the enemy and spilled your blood for the true cause of your kind...
You are finally ready.
As are we...

You see, child.
This... is where it ends.
Where we take back...what is ours.
No more waiting. No more hiding.
We are going...to show them. This land... is ***ours***. This ***world*** is ours.
In time we will...destroy each of the members of the Parliament. Turn them to...blackened bones and dust.
One. By one...
But first...a ***declaration***...
A brand.
A fire...so bright...that all will see and know...that we...have returned...
To take back...what is ours. In the place... where this all began...

Wh-what does that mean? Where are we going?
Heh...oh, child...don't you see?

We are going back to *Texas*, boy...
And we are going to burn it to the ground.

Good, Perrianne. Good...

You are...
Evolving.
I don't understand. How I am able to do these--
Out loud, dear. If you don't mind.
Oh...I'm sorry.
I'm doing that too much these days.
Do not apologize for what you are. This is why you came to me, child.
To...burn the chaparral that has hidden what you are... Forced it to...cloak inside of your mind lest it be unleashed...
I was Coroña's shepard long ago. I taught him the bones.
Taught him to ***see*** without his own eyes.

To look through the eyes of vultures, right? To...possess them? Control them?
Will...will I be able to do that?
No. No, each Elder comes with their own gifts.
Mind. Power. Flight. Sight.
Sight?
Yes. It has been said that some may see the future...
But... I'm not an Elder.
...Are you not?
You were sired by one of the ancients. One of the oldest and deadliest of your kind...
Your lineage only once removed from the first...
And then... raised by only one of two fire-born in all of creation...
Perrianne... if you are not an Elder...
Then I fear perhaps you are something far more dangerous...

What does that mean? Fire-born? The first? I don't understand...I was sired by my grandfather... stolen from the Landry family in retaliation for--
No. That is just the beginning. But it is only one small chapter. You have much to do yet...
I know.
...
How?
How... do you think?
You are the mind reader here... Not I.
I can't read your mind.
I think you know that.
Then how? How do I know these things?
Tell me...
Because...
You can see the future...

Tell me then.
Tell me what you see. How does this all end?
How it began.
Fire.
And...your father...
...Which one?
Hehe...
Now that...
Is a good question...
FWOOSHH
Perry...

...Time to go.
What'd I tell you about talkin' to that loon?
She is not a loon. She knows things. Things **I** need to know.
Something is coming! I have felt it for months now. Ever since Greg left, something has been building and I need to know who and ***what I am*** if we are going to--
You're a little girl who don't know any better. That's all you need to--
No, I am not.

You get out of my head, young lady.

What is a fire-born vampire?
Who is Demus?

What are you hiding...

Johan...

BONG
BONG
Perry, I--

BONG
BONG

The bells. JV, the alarms... what is--
Well...that *"somethin'"* you was talking about?

"...I reckon it's here."

CHOK
CHOK
CHOK
CHOK
BONG
BONG

July!
I need my gun!!!
What?!

...Ah, fuck.
BONG
BONG

Come get the baby and bring my guns, we're being invaded!!!
What?!
Goddammit.

CHOK
CHOK
CHOK
CHOK

Alright, just stay behind me, Perry.
Whatever this is, we can--

What the...

They're... frozen...
How in the hell?

Let 'em go, Perry!
I... don't like... helicopters...
Hey!!! Dammit, I said let them go!!!
Look. Those things are built to kill. If they wanted us dead, we wouldn't be having this conversation...
Now... before you change their minds...
Drop it!!!
...Fine.
JV, you see what I'm seeing? That symbol...
Yeah. I see it...
What? What is happening?!

That's
Frost.

The Parliament is here.
Gentlemen!
It's been too long.

Now...I know there's been some rather unfortunate business between us.
I want you to know that as far as the Parliament goes, that's water under the bridge. You have my word that--
That's far enough.

You listen to me. You'd do well to hop back on that bird and see yourself out. I believe my family and I have made it perfectly clear where we stand with all you people.
You say it's water under the bridge? Good. Keep it that way. I ain't got nothing' to say to y'all.

Now, now. JV, like I said...we come in peace.
I assure you, you're safe. We didn't come to pick a fight.

You're assurin' us? Well...that's awfully Christian of you. Only problem is...

You don't seem to understand where the hell you are, Frost...

CHCH
CHCH
CHCK
CH
You're in my town.
You wanna leave it alive...
I'd adjust your tone.
Okay...
Can... can we go somewhere to speak in private?

I think you'll want to hear what I have to say...

What the fuck am I looking at?

Is that a goddamn dragon?

That is drone footage we obtained from Demus's castle. It would appear he's done biding his time.
They're building something. Something big. We have a source on the inside, but we've lost contact after his last communique.
I...Jesus... one of these days y'all need to sit me down and give me a goddamn book report on who the hell this guy is.
We can get you anything you need.

...JV...
Anything you wanna add here? Awfully quiet there, chief...

Waiting to hear what the fuck this has to with any of us...

Well...that's just it, Johann.
I'm afraid it has everything to do with you and your family...

Bartlett...if you'll just flip to the next--
Jesus Christ...
JV...

He's back...

The hell are you talking about? Give me that, I can't--

No...

That's-that's impossible...

We had our suspicions. Seems he was rescued after his attack on Sulphur Springs.
Saved by his sire. By Demus. Listen to me, Johan...
We need your help. Your family's help. He is going to start a war that humanity cannot win. That we cannot win.
You were there for the last wars. You know how to--

Are you out of your fucking mind, Frost?!
NGH!
Are you so fucking scared that you came back here? To me! To my family?! You want me to suddenly forget what you did to us?!
All of a sudden, we're good enough for you, *huh?!* *Huh?!*
Answer me!
Because...
We... can't beat him without you...
He's going back to Texas, JV. Where this all started...

He's...he's going to destroy everything we have built.
The peace. The survival of our kind...

AGH!
How can I trust you?
How do I know I'm not walking into one of your bullshit Parliament games?
You don't think I would have come here without proof?
Give me a little credit.

This intel comes from a very reliable source.
I think you'll understand once you see...

How do you think we gathered all this intel?
You see, JV...

We have a man on the inside.

Months ago...
"I'm sure you have questions.

"Your son is lucky.
"He may not think so...
"And you very well may agree...
"But Gregory is lucky that we got to him...
Ah. Finally...
"Before the devil came for his due..."
Welcome to the Parliament of Vampires. I am sure you have heard of us.
My name is Frost.
Guards, you may remove the restraints.
Now, before we begin, I would like to--
Why don't you spare me the bullshit and tell me why the fuck I'm here?
...
Very well.

You are here, Gregory Bowman...
Because you killed an Elder.
Mmm. I thought that might grab your attention...
But you can relax. For now.
Vampire law lists one punishment, and one alone, for the intentional death of an Elder vampire.
And as loathsome as Carroña was...
Well... what are we without laws, yes?
So.
Consider yourself dead.
Wh-what is this?
That...is the report of your capture and execution that I will be sending to the rest of the council.
I don't understand...
Well, for one, Carroña was a maniacal psychotic who would have no doubt died by this council's hand one day...
But...
More to the point...I have uses for you.
You see...

There are larger threats at play.
Who... I mean... what is--
Demus.
The first, and most powerful, of our kind.
A fire-born vampire.
Like your father.

What?
What does that mean?
You will learn. I promise.
In time you will learn more than you ever wanted to know...
Wait...
Just... just hold on. No...
Why am I here? I don't--
Wait...
You--you said there was only one punishment for killing an Elder...
My dad and my uncle killed my grandpa...
He was an Elder too, right?
So...why aren't *they* dead?
Well, now...
The answer to that...
Is precisely why I have called you here...

From there it was a simple process of placing Greg in a position where he could be "*rescued*" by your father.
Since then he has been providing invaluable information on Demus and his--

Stop talking.

Bartlett? Take Perry and leave this room.

So...you want to speak alone. I can understand that.
My apologies if my–ahem–disclosure was too much for the girl. I had assumed she was of an age that she be informed.
But... yes. I agree. Discretion is perhaps best.
Shall I have my security leave then, as well?
No.
They can stay.

You sent my son!
AGH!

My only son!
He--he was--going--anyway--

AGGGHHHH!!

That seems to be going well.
Yup.
You should move your chair.
Huh? Why would I--

BOOOM!

Now... Johan, please, we can--
Shut up.
I'll help you. We all will. I'll go to war. This last time.
We'll burn out every inch of evil that's out there in the darkness you need burned.
But if anything happens to my son...
You, and every last one of your kind, will see who I am when I'm set loose.
And it'll be the last thing you ever see.

Oh-Okay... yes.
But...as much as you want to extract Greg, we can't take that castle. Not yet.
It's too dangerous.
Not what I was thinking...
JV, no...we can't--
It's been too long, Bartlett. I ain't having it. Go get ready. Get Evil and tell him to get gunned up.
This piece of shit wants to start a war in Texas...

"Let's give 'em one."

"And so...
"We have come full circle...
"We end...
"Where we began..."
NOW ENTERING
TEXAS
THE LONE STAR
STATE

There is only one lesson to be learned now...
Soon, the war will commence.
Soon... there will be fire.
And blood.
The Parliament... Frost and his ilk...we will face them.
And we will destroy them.
And we will finally take back...what is rightfully ours...
We will take this land. These... people...
Our hordes will once again blot out the sun...

Gregory...

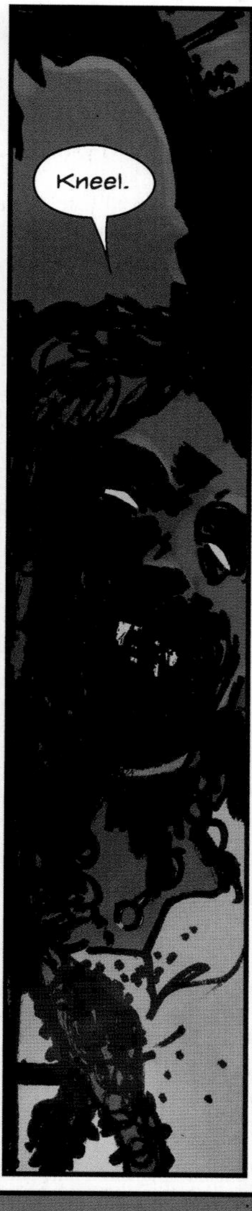
Kneel.

When you arrived here...
You were captured in possession...

Of an artifact.

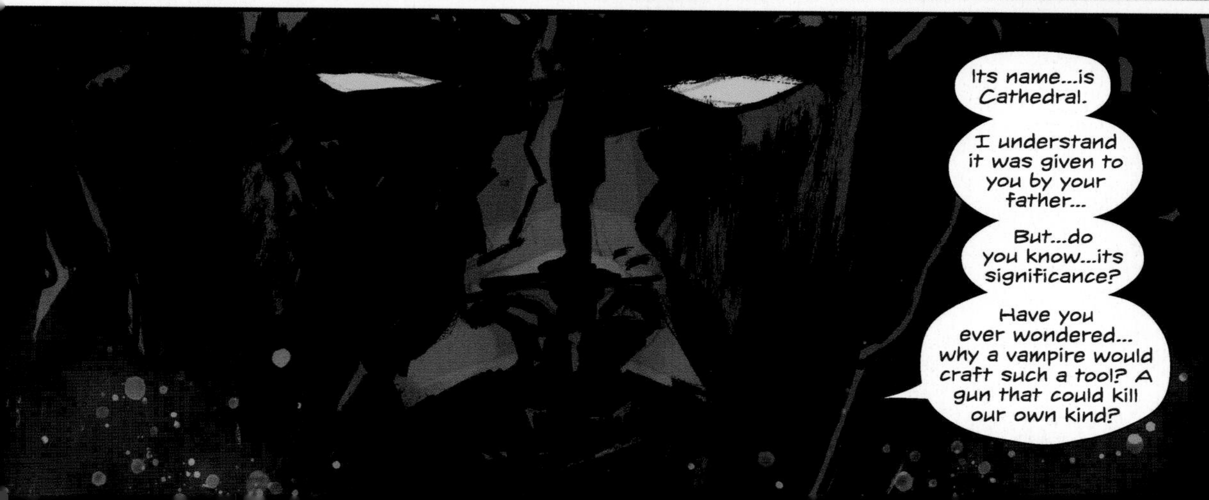
Its name...is Cathedral.
I understand it was given to you by your father...
But...do you know...its significance?
Have you ever wondered... why a vampire would craft such a tool? A gun that could kill our own kind?

Do you know its story?
N-no... no, Master... I do not...

When the first Parliament was made...
When your grandfather, your father, myself and our tribe first came to this land...

There was a certain... sect...of our kind...
Vampires. Among us...that tried to...rise up. To wrestle control... from me, and mine...
We destroyed them.

We... barricaded them in a cathedral. In consecrated ground.

And as their...bodies burned...the cathedral burned as well...
And from the melted steel of the church steeple... I forged *this*.

Do you know why?

No...
I don't. I don't understand--

It is a reminder.
A tool... used to kill those of our kind...

Agh!!! N-No! Wait!

...That betrayed us.

Oh... child...
Did you really think... I wouldn't know?

P-please... they-they gave me no choice...I-- I'm sorry! Please don't--
Shhh... hush now.

I know.
I know how they work... how the Parliament... how they use our kind...
Use us against each other...

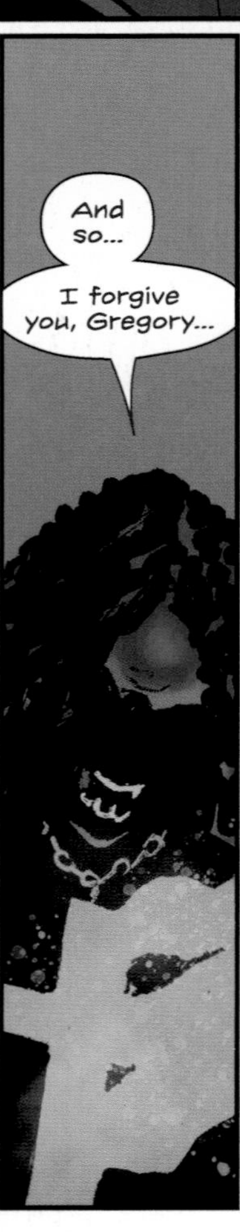
And so...
I forgive you, Gregory...

And I release you...

You see... I want him to know. Your father.
I want him to know our plans.

For you see, you have a part to play in this story yet, my child.

You will send your father a message. From me.
You will show him...my conviction.

Okay...
Th-thank you.

I will tell him. I'll-I'll tell them what you have told me.
No...

I'll tell him myself.

To be continued...

“We have come full circle…

We end where we began.”

FOR MORE TALES FROM *ROBERT KIRKMAN* AND *SKYBOUND*

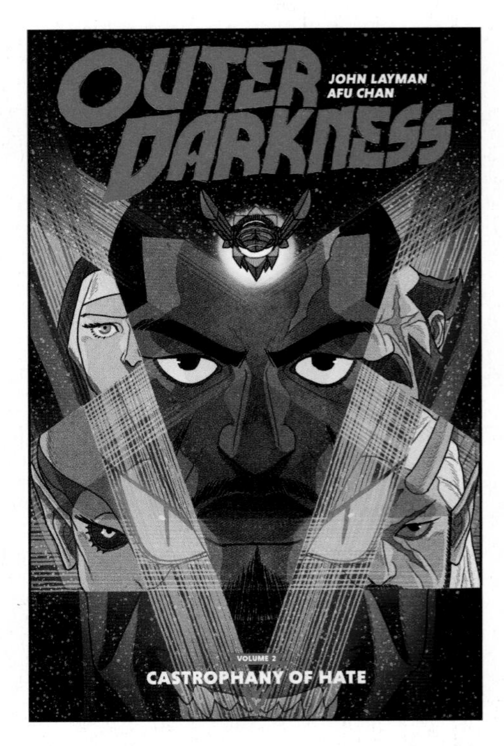

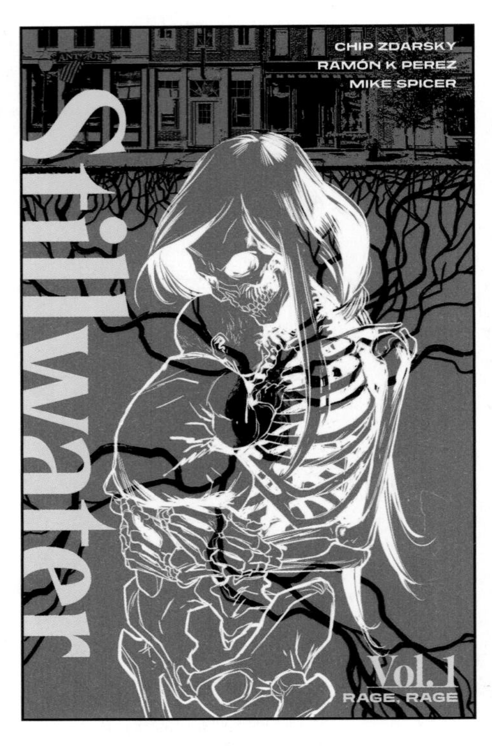

VOL. 1: EACH OTHER'S THROATS TP
ISBN: 978-1-5343-1210-4
$16.99

VOL. 1: CASTROPHANY OF HATE TP
ISBN:978-1-5343-1370-5
$16.99

VOL. 1: RAGE, RAGE TP
ISBN: 978-1-5343-1837-3
$16.99

VOL. 1: KILL THE PAST TP
ISBN: 978-1-5343-1362-0
$16.99

VOL. 2: THE PRESENT TENSE TP
ISBN: 978-1-5343-1862-5
$16.99

VOL. 1: BIENVENIDOS TP
ISBN: 978-1-5343-0506-9
$16.99

VOL. 2: FIESTA TP
ISBN: 978-1-5343-0864-0
$16.99

VOL. 3: VIVA MEXICO TP
ISBN: 978-1-5343-1231-9
$16.99

VOL. 1: FLORA & FAUNA TP
ISBN: 978-1-60706-982-9
$9.99

VOL. 2: AMPHIBIA & INSECTA TP
ISBN: 978-1-63215-052-3
$14.99

VOL. 3: CHIROPTERA & CARNIFORMAVES TP
ISBN: 978-1-63215-397-5
$14.99

VOL. 4: SASQUATCH TP
ISBN: 978-1-63215-890-1
$14.99

VOL. 5: MNEMOPHOBIA & CHRONOPHOBIA TP
ISBN: 978-1-5343-0230-3
$16.99

VOL. 6: FORTIS & INVISIBILIA TP
ISBN: 978-1-5343-0513-7
$16.99

VOL. 1: A DARKNESS SURROUNDS HIM TP
ISBN: 978-1-63215-053-0
$9.99

VOL. 2: A VAST AND UNENDING RUIN TP
ISBN: 978-1-63215-448-4
$14.99

VOL. 3: THIS LITTLE LIGHT TP
ISBN: 978-1-63215-693-8
$14.99

VOL. 4: UNDER DEVIL'S WING TP
ISBN: 978-1-5343-0050-7
$14.99

VOL. 5: THE NEW PATH TP
ISBN: 978-1-5343-0249-5
$16.99

VOL. 6: INVASION TP
ISBN: 978-1-5343-0751-3
$16.99

VOL. 7: THE DARKNESS GROWS TP
ISBN: 978-1-5343-1239-5
$16.99

THE ENTHUSIAST'S GUIDE TO DIY PHOTOGRAPHY

64 Projects, Hacks, Techniques, and Inexpensive Solutions for Getting Great Photos

MIKE HAGEN

HUSIAST'S GUIDE TO DIY PHOTOGRAPHY: ROJECTS, HACKS, TECHNIQUES, AND E SOLUTIONS FOR GETTING GREAT PHOTOS

Mike Hagen

The Enthusiast's Guide to DIY Photography
64 Projects, Hacks, Techniques, and Inexpensive Solutions for Getting Great Photos
Mike Hagen
www.VisAdventures.com

Project editor: Maggie Yates
Project manager: Lisa Brazieal
Marketing manager: Mercedes Murray
Copyeditor: Maggie Yates
Layout and type: WolfsonDesign
Cover design: WolfsonDesign
Indexer: Maggie Yates
Front cover image: Mike Hagen

ISBN: 978-1-68198-294-6
1st Edition (1st printing, December 2017)

Rocky Nook Inc.
1010 B Street, Suite 350
San Rafael, CA 94901
USA

www.rockynook.com

Distributed in the U.S. by Ingram Publisher Services
Distributed in the UK and Europe by Publishers Group UK

Library of Congress Control Number: 2017949800

This book is printed on acid-free paper.
Printed in China